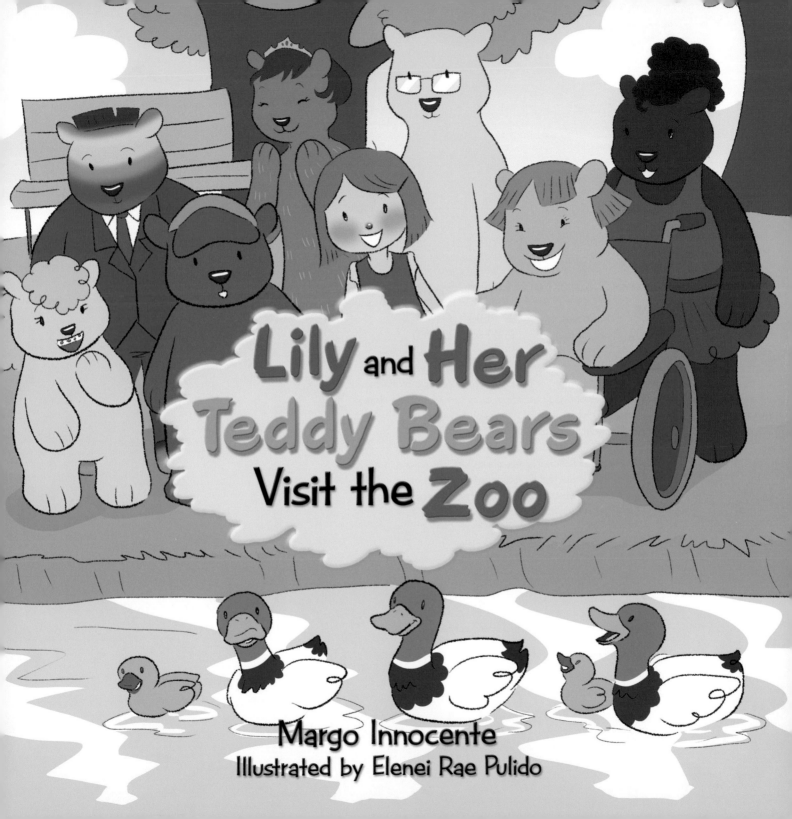

Lily and Her Teddy Bears Visit the Zoo

Margo Innocente

Illustrated by Elenei Rae Pulido

To order additional copies of this book, contact:
Xlibris
1-888-795-4274
www.Xlibris.com
Orders@Xlibris.com

Lily and Her Teddy Bears Visit the Zoo

This book is dedicated to Lily Collins for helping me realize that children become emotionally involved in the stories they read.

There once was a little girl named Lily who loved teddy bears. She had big ones, little ones, all different colored ones. Lilys' bears went everywhere with her.

One day Lily noticed that her teddy bears did not seem quite themselves, they appeared to be bored. Lily thought long and hard about what to do. She decided to take them on a trip to the zoo
Lily gathered all her bears together and told them the great news.
We are going to the zoo! She shouted!

After arriving at the zoo, the big question was "what to do first ". All the bears had their own ideas. Lily placed them all in a circle and did inny minny miney moe. The winner of the big decision was Lily of course. She picked the bunny cages!

On their way to the bunny cages, they came across a Lion cub who looked very sad. It seems the lion cub was lost, he could not find his mother. Lily and the bears assured the lion cub that there was nothing to fear, she and her teddy bears would help the little cub find his way back to his mother.

Lily and her bears came up with a plan to help this sad lion cub; the first thing to do was look for clues. Together as a team, they would look for paw prints that matched that of a lion.

Suddenly, Brown bear screeched !!! "I found some prints" he said! They were the paw prints from the lion cub. Yellow bear wondered how this could help us since we already knew where the lion cub was. Lily explained that they could follow the lion cub's prints back to where he started. So off they went after a long trail they came upon a mother lion looking very concerned. The mother lion turned and saw her lion cub and dashed into his arms! The two of them were so happy to be reunited that they forgot all about Lily and her bears.

Now it was time to find the bunny cages. As they walked, Red bear stopped. Red bear looked around and asked, "Does anyone hear that?"

Lily and the other bears listened very carefully. Suddenly they heard a soft chirp coming from above. As they all looked up, they noticed a baby bird sitting on a tree branch, Lily hollered up to the little bird asking what was wrong. The little bird admitted that he was too scared to fly so he could not play with his friends.

Lily and her bears thought for a moment and came up with a solution. Lily took an umbrella out of her backpack and handed it to Orange bear. Orange bear climbed up the tree to the branch that the little bird was pirched on and told the little bird to climb onto her back.

Orange bear opened the umbrella and jumped down from the tree floating to the ground. On their way down, the bird fell off in a panic he started to flap his wings. The little bird realized he was actually flying and shouted to his bird friends, and joined them in a game of tag.

The teddy bears wondered if they could continue on to the bunny cages. As Lily and her bears began to walk toward the bunny cages, they noticed a family of ducks in a pond nearby.

There was a mommy duck, a daddy duck, and seven ducklings. The Pink bear asked if they could feed the ducks. Lily agreed, she pulled bread out of the backpack, which was left over from their lunch. Lily and her bears threw bread into the water, piece by piece. The duck family ate until their tummies were full.

"Oh Boy!" said green bear, "Do you suppose we could go to the bunny cages now?" Everyone thought this was a great idea so off they went. Once the bunny cages were in full sight, Lily stopped suddenly.

Knowing that they finally made it, Lily was not as excited as she hoped to be. Lily and her bears waited all day to see the bunnies, they helped animals along the way, it was a great day so far, so why wasn't Lily feeling happy? Lily explained to her bears that she just wished her family could have shared in the fun.

Lily and her bears finally made it to the bunny cages. As they watched the bunnies hop around, Lily remembered all the great things that happened that day. Lily and her bears helped a lion cub return home to his mother, they helped a little bird learn to fly, and they fed a hungry family of ducks. What could make this day any better?

As Lily and her bears trotted off to see the rest of the zoo, Rainbow bear looked up only to see Lily's family approaching them. Rainbow bear tapped Lily on her shoulder pointing in the direction of her family. Lily noticed and expressed joy as she ran into her mother's arms, squeezing her so tight as she told her about her exciting day with her bears!! Lily, her bears, and her family finished the day at the zoo together.

Everyone including all the animals in the zoo were Happy.

Printed in the United States
By Bookmasters